A special dedication of love.
To my supportive darling mother Evelyn Henson.
Through your perseverence, strength, and family devotion
I found myself and became who I am today...

Mr. Sunny Sunshine
Prince of happiness, King of smiles.

Thank you mom!

To order additional copies of this book, contact:
Xlibris
1-888-795-4274
www.Xlibris.com
Orders@Xlibris.com

Discover the inspirational magic created from
smiles through the guidance of Mr. Sunny Sunshine.

Meet Mr. Sunny Sunshine Discover the
Magic of a Rainbow and a Smile.
Written and Illustrated
by
Dwayne S. Henson

1

Today as I took a good look into the mirror I ask myself what did I see? I saw a bright smile reflecting back at me, a happy bright smile, a smile that seemed to be pasted on to me. As I thought and wondered to myself, I said I'm glad a smile is another happy part of me.

Suddenly, from out of nowhere a rainbow appeared and came down and touched me. I said to myself, how could this be? This must be magic that I see. How could a rainbow come down and touch me?

With a smile and a face
full of joy I didn't know
what to say or what to do.

I began to wonder curiously, what else could this rainbow do? Can I have fun with it too?

Suddenly, to my surprise a rainbow appeared in my mind with a bright new rainbow idea.

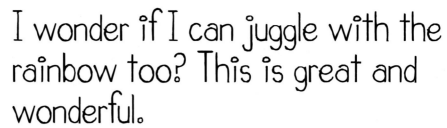

10

Hey! I just got a great idea.
I can put on my own show of
course with the help of my new
friend the rainbow.

I'll be Mr. Sunny Sunshine and my bright colorful assistant will be my newfound friend the rainbow. So look out world, here we come. We're getting ready to help everyone smile with a happy glow.

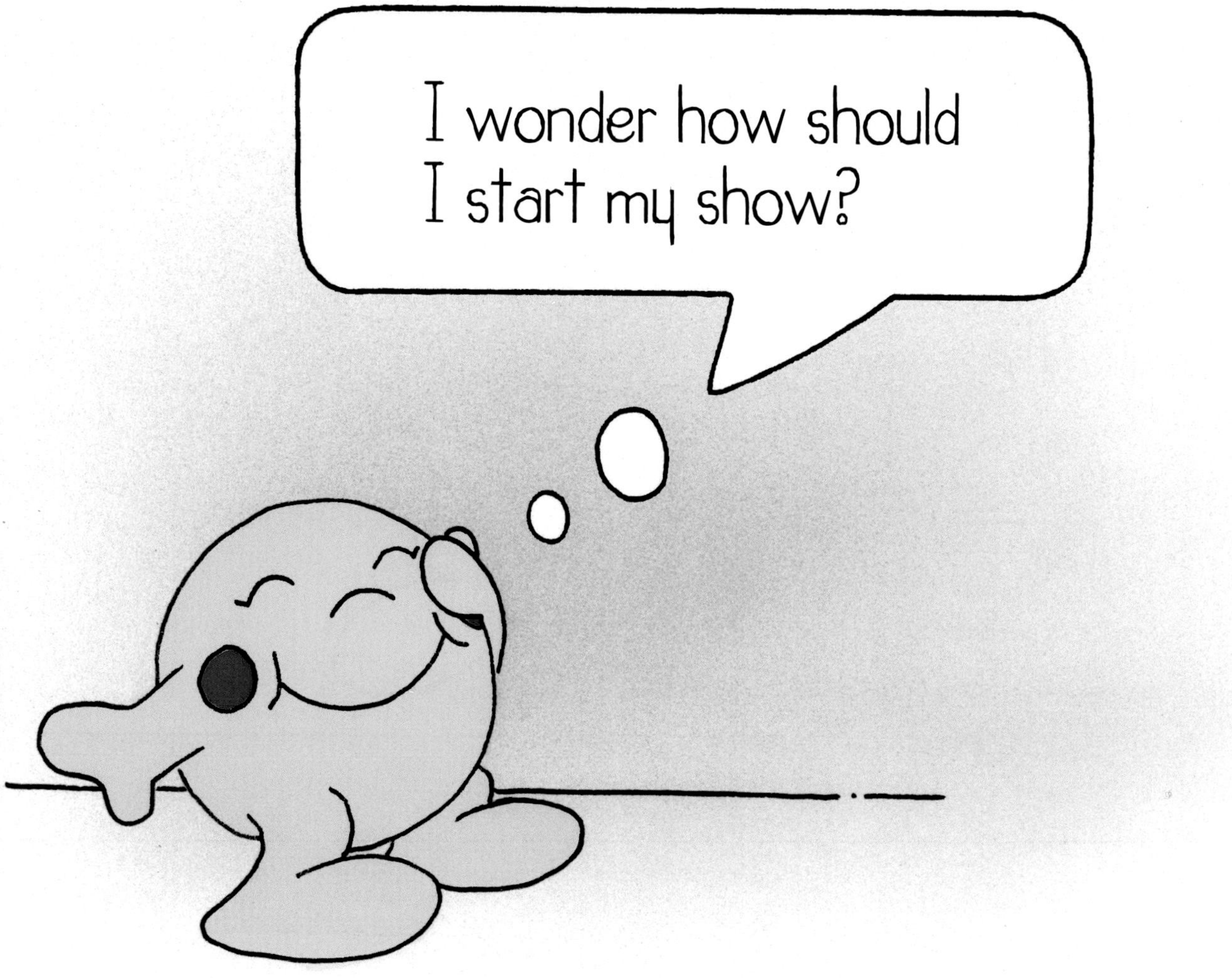
I wonder how should
I start my show?

20

25

What's a day without a smile?

Next a special offer and a preview of more
up coming Mr. Sunny Sunshine books. ⟶

A special offer from
the author / illustrator of the
Mr. Sunny Sunshine books
Dwayne S. Henson

Here's my special offer. Two preschool educational books combined in one at one regular sales price.

For more information on this special offer and other Mr. Sunny Sunshine books Contact Xlibris at: 1-888-795-4274

Dwayne S. Henson
Creator of Mr. Sunny Sunshine™

My gift that I would like to share with others is to inspire those who are in need of a smile and to educate others of the positive inspirational value that smiles provide in our society.

With Mr. Sunny Sunshine™ as my tool in this never ending educational smile-based journey. I aim to demonstrate how smiles can be utilized in so many positive encouraging ways such as to inspire, motivate, educate as well as to entertain. How Mr. Sunny Sunshine™ creates smiles and shares them with others, I truly believe, are some of the fascinating trademark dynamics of this inspiring smile making concept.

As you may come to discover there's more inspirational magic behind a smile than what we generally see.

From this unique unit of books you'll learn how and why Mr. Sunny Sunshine™ took it upon himself to create more smiles and inspiration all over the world. Along with this you'll also be provided with a one-of-a-kind, entertaining, smile-based education and much, much, more.

There's a lot to uncover and learn about a smile. I invite you to journey along to see how truly motivating a smile can be.

I certainly hope you enjoy my Mr. Sunny Sunshine™ books as much as I did creating them for others to share. I look forward to creating lots more smiles for many of years to come.

Sincerely, Dwayne S. Henson... Prince of happiness, King of smiles.

Printed in the United States
By Bookmasters